The Arachnoid Man

The Arachnoid Man

Allen Matthews

ISBN-13: 9781544239941
ISBN-10: 1544239947
Library of Congress Control Number: 2017903770
CreateSpace Independent Publishing Platform
North Charleston, South Carolina

Preface

THE ARACHNOID MAN is a short story which chronicles the explicit romantic/sexual exploits and journey of a man who was previously a sickly child whose life was transformed by the sting of a mysterious arachnoid scorpion. He grew up to become the arachnoid man, the lawyer, law enforcer, author, private detective and one endowed with great sexual prowess. Welcome to his world, learn and enjoy the read.

The Story

⸺ ❧ ⸺

THE BEGINNING OF the story is set in the northeast of England in a town called Hull. Early one winter morning, at about two o'clock, a thirteen-year-old boy named Douglas was awoken from sleep by the sting of an arachnoid arthropod: a mysterious scorpion. On waking to consciousness, he saw the scorpion crawling away backward calmly and majestically and looking directly into his eyes as though sending him a message. For about five minutes, he felt paralyzed; it was as though his brain and spinal cord were on fire, with a flaming red-hot steel thrust into his brain, and as if things were being downloaded into his brain and body. Thereafter, a sense of peace, great serenity, and strength surged through his whole body, and he felt completely transformed. He gradually drifted back to sleep, but on waking up the next morning, he was a changed boy. He began to develop supernatural strengths, beauty, and unique attributes. It was as though electricity were flowing through his veins. He was no longer sickly and lethargic. A genetic transformation had taken place; he had unique brain powers, insight, confidence, calmness, and great courage. He learned very fast and read faster. His speech was succinct and eloquent, and he knew the contents of books he had never read. His skin glowed with a shine of immortality. For both his family and his schoolmates, there was no mistaking it: he was now a changed and transformed boy. Gone were the days of sickness and feebleness. On one occasion, the bullies came at him as usual on the playground. A gentle push sent one of them flying through the air. With their jaws dropped, the others quietly walked away one after another. They left him alone forever, as they noticed he was a changed boy. On learning about his experience with the scorpion, they named him the arachnoid boy.

The arachnoid boy became the arachnoid man, who studied law and philosophy at the university, graduating with distinction. Upon graduation he joined the metropolitan police as an officer because he was passionate about justice, law, and order and he wanted to make a difference to his community. He was a strong, well-mannered, tall, eloquent, stylish, and elegant man, but he remained unmarried. Many women fell for him, wanting offspring with his attributes, but his mutation due to the sting could not be inherited. Most of his children rather inherited the early-childhood sickly defects that were initially characteristic of him.

A group of five women who had eight children with the arachnoid man brought a class suit against him, claiming that their children were sickly and feeble instead of possessing the strong and admirable qualities they saw in him. They were also suing for more child support.

The lawsuit was highly publicized and serialized in one of the major tabloid newspapers. One of the women, named Ela, who had one child with the arachnoid man, testifying in the witness box, said he had done nothing wrong, his position was clear from the outset of their relationship, and she had the best sex ever with him; he was the only man she had been with who made her feel a whole woman by making her achieve multiple orgasms. Her disappointment was that her child with him lacked the strong qualities that he had, which was what had attracted her to him in the first place, and the money for childcare provided by the arachnoid man was suboptimal. Ela recounted the memory of the first night she met him, stating, "After a two-minute gaze from his deep-blue eyes into mine, I was somewhat aroused. My clitoris was tingling, and I could not resist the pull toward him, maybe partly because I was just coming out of a broken relationship in which I felt injured. The sex that night was unforgettable, with his well-sized rock-hard phallus in my pussy. While lying on his back, he rotated me in a sitting position, and with every one-hundred-eighty-degree rotation, he gave me a relishing, pounding penile thrust. During the rotations, it was as though all the nerve fibers in that area were ravaged with passion. I felt as if I were on cloud eleven. It was the best I have ever encountered. His erectile staying power is phenomenal. He is gentle and manly and has a disarming touch. He is also a decent man, never rough, rash, abrasive, or inconsiderate. Initially, I thought he was taking some erectile-enhancing performance pills, but he assured me he was not, and this was validated by the fact that when I turned up unannounced, his performance in bed was equally well sustained. My anger is that he insisted on using a condom because he did not want me to become pregnant, but I punctured the condom and became pregnant. I cannot forget, and I vividly remember the horrified expression on his face when he asked me where the ejaculum was, following the withdrawal of his penis, and I had to confess to him that I had punctured the condom. I was giggling, and he was fuming. It was the only occasion I have ever seen him mildly upset. In spite of that, he did not say any unkind or harsh words to me, for he is a man who has achieved mastery over himself and his circumstances."

Now it was Melissa's turn to take the witness stand. She claimed her child was the result of a good and deliberate one-night stand. "We met, and I invited him to my place after the show at the pub. It was hilarious. Six months earlier, after thirteen years of marriage, my husband had left me because I could not have a child. That night I got what I have always wanted, and I am not complaining; my baby is fine. The arachnoid man was good with his fingers, hitting my G-spot and clitoris simultaneously. He sent me through the roof. He pressed the right buttons. Some men do not know their way around a woman's body. All of them need to learn the skill. Some are rough, raw, and uncultured. They need to be educated. His manhood was well endowed, of good length and thickness, and he had great erectile staying power even after the release. He could continue to pump strongly; that I enjoyed a lot. His energy was electromagnetic; his dick was like a vibrator, critically stimulating the whole area during the thrust. He was stronger than a stallion. He also rolled his tongue around my nipple with great dexterity, and he had good sucking power, adding to the overall ecstasy, euphoria, and romantic bliss. I can't complain. I had the best time of my life with him, and actually, I came to the stand to support him, because he has done nothing wrong. He made it clear to me—and as far as I am aware, to others as well—that he did not want marriage or children, because of his childhood experience, and that he could not guarantee that his children or offspring would have the same admirable qualities that drew us to him."

In the witness box, a tall, eloquent lady named Mandy said, "My husband left me after fifteen years of marriage, accusing me of frigidity and infertility. Thank God he left. For fifteen years I carried the guilt in ignorance, believing the lie, not knowing that it was the bastard who was infertile and ignorant of how to stimulate the erogenous areas in the female body. I was equally ignorant. I did not know I had a clitoris that could be stimulated. The arachnoid man is very good in bed and highly virile. Every man ought to learn from him; he must be in the top two percent. His ability to locate and stimulate the G-spot, a rough area in the anterior vaginal wall, with his finger running up and down, coupled with simultaneous stimulation of the clitoris with the fingers of the other hand, sent me through the clouds with ripples of ecstasy to achieve great multiple and satisfying female orgasms. I had sex with him only once before I became pregnant, after failing for fifteen years."

Interjecting, Judge Palmer said, "Save us the bedroom details, and concentrate on the relevant points."

Responding, Mandy retorted, "Your Lordship, sex and offspring go hand in hand; they are inseparable. I am going into detail to ensure a balanced view and to help the millions of silently suffering woman to be better informed. When I approached him, he made it clear to me he did not want children, because of his childhood experience of partial parental rejection because of his frequent illnesses. Partial parental rejection is worse than outright rejection because in outright rejection, the child knows where he or she stands, whereas in partial rejection, the child is confused, not knowing what to believe or embrace as to whether the parents hate or love him or her. At times they loved him or her like a saint while at other times they hated him or her like a devil. He told me if I had a baby, I was on my own in raising the child but he would be very willing to support me financially, and he has been faithful to his commitments in that regard. But an improved contribution would be welcome and is desirable."

Continuing, Mandy said, "I remember how during our first meeting, when he hooked up with me at the party, I wanted to turn him down because I felt his manhood would be too big for me to handle. After that first encounter, I was so satisfied and elated that we exchanged phone numbers and continued to see each other. This led to the birth of Jim. At that first encounter, he was so good, and he demonstrated a lot of prowess in the use of his fingers in my pussy; I came several times but never before. His manhood was just the right size and had great sustaining power, pounding me into ecstasy and making me moan with pleasure. I hope you understand where I am coming from, having been considered or described as frigid for fifteen years prior."

Ranjini, in the witness box, said, "In fairness to the arachnoid man, he never forced himself on me. I am more conservative and less prone to divulge the details of my sexual encounters with him, but I must say that sex with him gives me a perplexing, dreamlike sensory bliss whose joy lingers long after the event. His kiss is also tranquilizing, neither cold nor lifeless. In fairness to him, when I started a relationship with him and told him I wanted his baby so the child would have his good build and great characteristics, he made it clear to me that he has always told all the women coming to him with such expectations that he could not guarantee that their offspring would share his unique qualities. He was not born with those characteristics but developed them following his encounter with the arachnoid scorpion, so he does not know whether the changes can be inherited, and he has resisted medical testing to evaluate it. When the arachnoid man came into my life, I thought he would afford me the privilege of sharing a Mendelssohn's 'Wedding March' with him, but that was not to be. For him, that was a dream too farfetched, as he told me that marriage was out of the question as far as he was concerned."

In the witness box, Fiona testified that when their relationship started, the arachnoid man described to her the genesis of his transformation. It was traceable to the sting by an arachnoid scorpion by which he was awoken that early winter morning. "Before I met the arachnoid man, I had four children and never had an orgasm. As you can see, I am on the big side, so my pussy is also large. Since meeting him, I have lost count of the number of orgasms I have had during our encounters. He is good at thrusting his knee into my large pussy, giving me a good filling effect, leading to abundant ecstasy. The feeling is both electrifying and tranquilizing. His dexterity in body-to-body massage is wonderful. It sets my nerves tingling in all directions with a perturbing resonance of serenity. He came into my life at the right time, giving me all I wanted. He introduced me to kneeling, thumbing, fisting, toe thrusting, and heeling, all of which have a very good feeling and sensual effects that are otherwise difficult to achieve with a voluptuous woman."

Continuing, Fiona stated that the ecstasy was not one sided, as she also learned to give him very satisfying blow jobs. "The tip of his penis is very sensitive, and sucking it sends him wriggling in enjoyment as though in pain. I also made him enjoy breast relief over my large tits. He likewise enjoyed caressing my large, fatty thighs, fondling them into ripples like a wave.

"What I have against the arachnoid man is that when I started the relationship with him—which I admit was initiated by me—he was not as clear as he could have been to me that his offspring may not inherit his great attributes, and my expectation was very high. My first child with him was a disappointment, as he was sickly and feeble. The second is okay but does not seem to have inherited the arachnoid man's qualities and the characteristics I was expecting. I had them in quick succession, so I could not tell in the early months that my first baby with him would be very sickly. Otherwise, I would not have had a second child with him. In fairness to him, though, sex with him was very great and fulfilling. He is the only man who has always made me achieve several good orgasms in addition to squirting orgasms on every occasion. I think he should set up an institution where men can be educated about pressing and operating the right buttons in a female's body. That would make the world a better place for most women. Some of them suffer in silent deprivation till death. His use of his tongue on my neck and ear while he verbalizes some romantic words during his thrust is explosive. The thought of it alone sends shivers of good feelings down my spine. It is both hilarious and delicious. Some are advocating that women need a pink pill to enhance their libidos. I beg to differ. I think what they need are men who understand the female body and who know their way around it or what to do to always help women achieve orgasm. The pills have limitations and side effects and can turn out for some to be a cure that is worse than the problem. Many women are sick from lack of love and from sexual discontent. What they need is proper and skillful bedroom attention rather than pills. There are no frigid women. There are only ignorant, selfish, and impatient men who do not know what to do to arouse the female body, and they all need to learn from men like the arachnoid man."

The arachnoid man, being a lawyer, defended himself in the lawsuit. Starting, he said, "None of these relationships was initiated by me—no, not one—and I was never in two relationships at the same time. I respect women, and I never forced myself on anyone. I hold the view that no woman should be violated and that sex should be consensual. They came to me claiming they saw some qualities in me they liked and wanted. I made it clear to all of them I did not want children, because of my early-childhood experience. In those early days, I had a severe form of childhood asthma, and I was sickly." At this point the arachnoid man was in tears as the memories of those early days came flooding into his consciousness, and using his white handkerchief, he gently dabbed at the teardrops.

Continuing, he said, "My sister Evelyn was as strong as stone. She was hardly sick, but I was sick virtually every fortnight before my experience with the arachnoid scorpion at the age of thirteen. My parents thought I would not survive early childhood. They were of the opinion that I was born weak. My mother had to stop working to look after me. My parents made many sacrifices, but grudgingly; they made me feel it was my fault for being sickly. My mother had to stop working for seven years when I was between the ages of five and thirteen. That affected her career progression as a high school teacher, and she was very resentful of it. Dad was a national rail worker. We enjoyed train journeys a lot. Dad was a good man, but he was a distant influence because as a train driver, he traveled often. He was generous, though, toward the family. This is what informed my desire not to have children.

"The prerogative to decide to seek medical advice to evaluate whether my unique attributes or characteristics could be inherited was mine, and in choosing not to do so, I have done nothing wrong. Though I wanted no children, I have not shrunk from the responsibility of providing financially for all the children as well as I consider necessary. I have provided the court with all records of the payments I have made to justify this claim."

In concluding the case, Judge Palmer ruled that the arachnoid man was not guilty of any of the charges filed against him, and he was discharged and acquitted. Nonetheless, the judge added that as the arachnoid man was a man of great substance and wealth owing to the large royalties he got from his published books, he should significantly increase his child-support payments to the mothers, paying more attention to those whose children were sickly.

The result of the lawsuit was also well publicized in a national tabloid newspaper in full, headlined "The Strong Arachnoid Man Weeps in Court, Sexual Exploits Exposed, the Mighty Is Fallen."

The lawsuit generated so much publicity that it was thought that though the arachnoid man had been acquitted, it would be difficult for him to continue to function as a senior police officer, a role in which he had served with distinction for twenty-five years after graduating from university, where he studied law and philosophy as combined honors, finishing with a first class. He therefore took early retirement from the police force after the court case.

A retirement party was organized by the police force for the arachnoid man. It was well attended, as he was very much liked and well respected by his colleagues. During the celebration, some of them recounted their memories of service together with him and his ingenuity and exploits. One such officer was Chief Constable Lee, who recalled how during their days in the police academy, the arachnoid man had outstanding performance and was always immaculately dressed. Lee also recalled an occasion in class when the instructor asked a question he thought no one would be able to answer. To his surprise, the arachnoid man's answer made the instructor better informed about the subject. "Such was his level of understanding and grasp of details that it can be both mesmerizing and enchanting listening to him. Nonetheless, he does not flaunt his knowledge or make you feel less of a person because of it. He is the most well-rounded gentleman I have ever met."

Inspector Ben Jones, giving his speech at the occasion, recalled how they went to arrest a drug baron, with the arachnoid man leading the team, adding that the arachnoid man's insights were also instrumental in the sting operation that led to the evidence for the arrest. As they walked into the house following a forced entry, the drug baron was sitting on a red sofa with a cigar in one hand and a glass of whiskey in the other. "It was as though he was expecting us, as he offered neither resistance nor denial but bellowed out in a baritone voice, 'Every man has a price. Name yours, and I will more than match it.'

"The arachnoid man promptly responded by saying, 'Our integrity is not for sale.' That dissolved any hesitation on my part, so I quickly moved toward the drug baron, gently handcuffed him, and led him out of his mansion into the waiting police van. The reinforcement team stationed outside was not needed. The arachnoid man's departure from the force will no doubt create a vacuum that can hardly be filled. The drug baron was convicted, and he is still behind bars."

Adding his voice to the commendations, Superintendent Adam Smith said, "The arachnoid man has been one of the most invaluable officers I have ever worked with in my thirty-five years in the service. He is a good, poised, imperturbable officer who is largely responsible for the good administrative structure we have in place in this constabulary, in that he was instrumental in drafting most of our standard operating procedures, which have stood the test of time and enjoyed the support of all staff members. He is leaving behind a legacy of excellence. His knack for solving difficult criminal cases resulting in prosecutions is unsurpassed, and I am sure many examples will be narrated by other speakers who have worked more intimately with him in the field. His ability to diffuse tension is also incredible. The example that comes to my mind is an incident I will never forget, when an angry lone gunman burst into the station while I was manning the desk years ago. I was terrified, but somehow the arachnoid man successfully persuaded him not to shoot and to put his loaded gun on the floor. He said that he could give the gunman a personal assurance that his grievances against the force would be well addressed. Everybody present was greatly relieved that the incident ended peacefully. Such was his acumen in matters like that."

Commenting during the party, Commander Joel Maxwell said, "The arachnoid man is an officer who leads from the front and is not afraid to get in the firing line. He epitomizes courage and wisdom. On one occasion," he continued, "we came under a barrage of gunfire from the gang that we were scheduled to go arrest. Somehow the arachnoid man identified the group leader and instructed one of our marksmen to take him down. He said that if the leader was out of the equation, the others would stop shooting and give themselves up. True to his prediction, about two minutes later, the gang leader, in a green jacket, was down, and everything fell silent. The others gave themselves up and were duly arrested. Such is his skill, his ability to correctly read the situation and exercise the right judgment. He will be sorely missed."

Police Constable Jasper Evans said, "The arachnoid man meant everything to me: a father figure, a mentor, a brother, an adviser, and an instructor, holding me accountable at times. I lost my father at an early age, and ever since, I have been in search of a worthy father figure. This I found after meeting and knowing the arachnoid man. He has always been there for me. He was also at my wedding, and he is the godfather to our little son. I enjoy a great sense of inexplicable peace around him. He taught me to value time and never waste a day. Previously, I had confidence issues. Under his mentorship, I have grown to develop the boldness of a lion. What more can I say? He can rest assured that even though he is leaving the force, I intend to keep our relationship intact."

The last speaker, presenting a golden award for excellent service to the arachnoid man, was Police Commissioner Martin Crosby. He started by saying, "Let it be said loud and clear that the arachnoid man, Douglas Ronald Stafford, is leaving the service with his outstanding and excellent record untarnished. I have followed his recent court case with interest and rapt attention, and he has been found not guilty of all the charges brought against him. Nonetheless, in keeping with the man of integrity that he is, he is of the view that in light of the publicity generated by the court case, his ability to function in an unbridled manner in the public sphere has been compromised. Thus, he has opted to take an early retirement. Douglas, as I call him, more than deserves this golden award. Over the past twenty-five years, he has served in various capacities with distinction in an exemplary manner and in the spirit of excellence. When the annals of this constabulary are written, his achievements and contributions will stand out. His interpersonal relationship with both senior and junior staff is worthy of emulation. He is a man who is blessed with a great personal magnetism. His role as an instructor has been performed without blemish. His contributions to fighting crime as a field officer have solved many crimes, and he has in no small measure played a significant role in helping us avoid miscarriage of justice. An example that readily comes to mind is one in which the father was the initial suspect, but eventually we found out the abuser was the mother. His deep insight helped us pursue the appropriate lines of investigation and secure the conviction of the correct offender. The memories of his outstanding contributions and services will long remain very well treasured in the constabulary. He has confided in me that he intends to work as a private detective after his retirement, and I have no doubt whatsoever that he will be as outstanding in that career he has been with us. His wealth of experience in the police force will certainly be an advantage, and his personality, as well as his attributes, will help him to excel. We all wish him the very best in all his future endeavors. It now remains for me to decorate him with the Medal of Meritorious Long Service, which he more than very well deserves."

The retirement party ended with a cocktail party, during which, while everyone was eating and drinking, the police band played, and a comedian police officer interjected some comedy. The band played some of the arachnoid man's much-loved music by Sinatra, to which the arachnoid man danced with amazing dexterity and youthful flexibility, to the pleasant surprise of all present who had never seen him dance. Evelyn was the arachnoid man's dancing partner, and together they danced a waltz, which further astonished the crowd. This indeed was a joyous occasion for him, and he was savoring the moment to the fullest, especially after the strain of the court case. The arachnoid man was immaculately dressed for the occasion, wearing a white shirt with black stripes, a white tie, a red waistcoat, black trousers, a golden Rolex wristwatch, shining spotless white shoes, and a creamy partly silver glittering jacket with a white handkerchief emerging from the breast pocket.

The occasion was brought to an end by Detective Inspector Lucy Boyle proposing a toast for the future success and happiness of the arachnoid man.

A month after his retirement and setting up his private detective company, on a bright summer day, the arachnoid man received a phone call from a wealthy lady living in London, asking him to help resolve the case of the kidnapping of her seventeen-year-old daughter, named Yvonne, in which the kidnappers were demanding a five-million-pound ransom. Soon after the phone call from Baroness Betty Cardwell, the arachnoid man dressed up and headed for her house to obtain a detailed interview with her and learn more about the circumstances of her daughter's kidnapping. As the arachnoid man got into his elegant white Porsche Cayenne, many thoughts began to agitate his mind: the thought that this was the first case he would handle in his capacity as a private detective and that it was crucial for him, the image and reputation of his company, and his profile to do things right, get things right, and duly resolve the case without loss of life.

As he stepped out of his car into a beautiful, well-paved driveway, Baroness Betty Cardwell was already waiting to receive him into her mansion home, but the grim anxiety written all over her face could not be disguised. She looked like a broken and helpless woman. While in her large lounge, she asked the arachnoid man to take a seat as she began to tell him about her daughter's kidnapping. "She was taken shortly after leaving the gym. She usually goes to the gym after school before coming home. It was unusual of her not to be home by six o'clock. On realizing that she was not home by eight, I began to wonder and tried to contact her, but the call went to her voice mail. At eight thirty, the kidnappers called using her phone and demanded a five-million-pound ransom, warning that if I valued her life, I should not mess around or get the police involved. They gave me instructions as to how to deliver the money."

The arachnoid man inquired, "Were you allowed to talk to her?"

"Yes," Baroness Betty replied. "She was distraught and was crying on the phone. I tried to comfort and reassure her as best I could. While I was talking to her, the kidnappers were threatening in the background in muffled bass and tenor voices. They eventually snatched the phone from her as she was sobbing, and they warned me to follow their instructions without deviating, after which they switched off the phone."

The arachnoid man asked Baroness Betty whether she had a sense of how many kidnappers were there.

"I am not absolutely sure," she replied, "but my guess from the background talk I was hearing is that they are three."

"Could you guess the ages?" he inquired.

"No, not at all," came her sobbing reply.

"Who else lives in this house apart from you and your daughter?"

"My friend Ben Slate also lives here," said Baroness Betty. "He moved in about three years ago, after I lost my husband, Yvonne's dad, five years ago following a sudden heart attack. Ben and Yvonne do not get on well at all. They are poles apart, like water and fire. They disagree on virtually every issue. I wonder whether Ben had a hand in the kidnapping, espe-cially since the kidnappers seem to have a good knowledge of her daily routine. In addition, Ben has not been as empathetic as I expected, and he appears indifferent to my plight and has been avoiding eye contact with me of late. I also know that though Ben has many good sides to him, he is a greedy man who would not care about violating others to make money, even at the expense of loved ones. I am suspicious that he had a hand in the kidnapping, though I have no proof."

"Is Ben at home now? I would like to have a word with him," the arachnoid man asked.

"No, he is not at home now," replied Baroness Betty.

"Can you please give me his phone number so I can call him later?"

"Yes, of course," she replied, fetching her phone from her red bag to find his number. "I am not good at memorizing phone numbers." She eas-ily found his number and called it out as the arachnoid man made an effort to record it on his gold-plated iPhone.

Rising to his feet, the arachnoid man said, "I will call Ben later for a chat. Please kindly notify him I will be calling him. In the meantime I will start working on a strategy to resolve this kidnapping and get your daugh-ter back to you safely. I will visit the gym and the site of the kidnapping. That will help me to better piece things together and to locate where they might be holding her. Can you give me Yvonne's phone number as well? For now, my position is, we are not paying any ransom. If that position changes, I will inform you immediately."

After several attempts the arachnoid man was able to speak on the phone to Ben Slate the next day. Following a long interrogation, he con-cluded that Ben had no hand in Yvonne's kidnapping even though his phone record registered unanswered calls from a mobile phone we later knew the kidnappers were using a few days prior to the kidnapping. That same phone was used to contact Yvonne on several occasions one to two weeks before her kidnapping.

The arachnoid man visited the site of Yvonne's abduction and, based on his ability of clairvoyance, was able to pinpoint the address where

Yvonne was being held. The landlord of the house was contacted for questioning as to who rented the property and the occupants. He said the tenant was a young man in his early thirties and that two evenings ago three males, including the tenant, and a young female, as seen on the CCTV recording, went into the flat and had not come out since then. After establishing that the young lady on the CCTV recording was Yvonne, the arachnoid man instructed two of his personnel to maintain round-the-clock surveillance of the building. The next day, about eighty hours after the kidnapping, the arachnoid man and some armed police stormed the apartment at three o'clock in the morning. The kidnappers were caught unaware as they were all awoken by the bang of the noisy police entry.

They were handcuffed and led away into waiting police vans. The apartment was littered with cans of beer, cigarette butts, and illicit drugs. After detailed and separate interrogations of the kidnapping suspects, they all gave the same story, indicating that it was Yvonne, wanting to extort some money from her millionaire mum, who had hatched the plan for her kidnapping. Yvonne strongly felt that it would work out well and that because her mum loved her, she would pay within forty-eight hours, and Yvonne would give them their own cut. But unknown to Yvonne, their plot was that if they got the money, they would double-cross her and merely release her without giving her any of it. They were planning to keep it all for themselves. The numerous phone calls and the content of the conversations between Yvonne and her kidnappers confirmed their story.

They claimed it was Yvonne who gave them Ben Slate's phone number to incriminate him and draw attention away from her, but though they called the number several times before and after the kidnapping, he never responded to their calls.

A few days after the foiled kidnapping, with Yvonne back at home, the arachnoid man called her on the phone to question her about her role in her kidnapping and confronted her with the kidnappers' side of the story. He also told her about the several phone records of her contacts with them prior to the kidnapping as well as the details of her conversations with them and her ploy to incriminate her stepfather.

In light of his investigation findings, the arachnoid man arranged a meeting with Baroness Betty and her daughter, Yvonne, to be held at their home. At the meeting the arachnoid man explained that the investigatory findings pointed to the fact that Yvonne was central to planning and orchestrating her own kidnapping and that she had admitted this to him. On hearing this, Baroness Betty was at first speechless. Her hands began to tremble uncontrollably, but she soon regained her composure and gathered herself. Thereafter, the disgust and disbelief on her face soon melted into compassion and love for Yvonne. She rose up from her sitting position on a brown three-seater and moved toward Yvonne, who was sitting opposite her. Embracing Yvonne, she started crying and muttering, "I do not know what I have done as your mother to deserve this, but as your mother, I still love you, and I forgive you."

Yvonne was now also in tears. With their heads on each other's shoulders, Yvonne replied, saying, "Mum, you have done nothing to deserve me doing this to you. I was the one who went off the rail, and I am deeply sorry, and I am ashamed of myself." After further sobbing, they both assumed their former sitting positions while wiping away their tears. All the while the arachnoid man just sat watching, with his right hand held over his chin.

Following a moment of silence, the arachnoid man interjected. "The question now, Baroness Betty, is whether we should charge and prosecute the kidnappers, knowing full well that if we do, Yvonne will go down with them."

After sitting motionless for a while, as though lost in thought, Baroness Betty bellowed, "Yvonne is all I have. I lost my husband"—she pointed to his picture on the wall—"and I will not lose Yvonne. I cannot have her stand trial or be imprisoned. If that means the kidnappers walking away free, so be it, but warn them never to come close to her again." She pointed fiercely with her right index finger as she ended her sentence.

The arachnoid man said, "If that is what you want, that is what will happen." He stood up and began to make his way out of Baroness Betty's mansion.

Baroness Betty, with an outstretched hand, said, "Thank you very much for your competent handling of the case and for affording me the outcome I wanted. Before approaching you, I had implicit confidence in your ability to resolve the issue. Now that confidence has been reinforced. Please kindly send me your invoice, and I will be effecting payment without delay."

Bowing in acknowledgment, the arachnoid man calmly walked out. Seated in his light-blue Bentley Bentayga, the arachnoid man looked toward the building as he pressed the ignition button. With a smile, he waved to Baroness Betty and Yvonne, who were now standing side by side at the entrance of their mansion home. They waved in return. Betty held Yvonne's hand as they turned to go into the lounge while the arachnoid man drove away. As he drove away, he was filled with a mixture of relief, excitement, and fulfillment that his first assignment as a private detective had had a successful outcome.

The kidnappers were released without charge and received only a police caution.

A week later, the arachnoid man received a message by e-mail and text requesting him to help investigate the sudden and suspicious death of a prominent Nigerian oba in Yorubaland, as the police were not making any headway in resolving the mystery. The toxicology report following a postmortem examination confirmed that the oba had died of poisoning. The initial attempts by the police to find the culprit were futile; therefore, the palace administrator, Ola Bada, who had been educated at Manchester University, had contacted the arachnoid man for help. It was rumored that the palace administrator or one of the oba's four wives was responsible for the poisoning; thus, the palace administrator was bent on finding out the truth. Sure of his innocence, he did not want his name soiled unduly, as he had been very loyal to the oba.

The arachnoid man started packing his suitcase for the Nigeria trip. He was unsure about the kind of clothing he would require. This is his first international contractual assignment as a private detective, and he was going to a country he had never visited, but he was not the kind of person to be deterred by such fears. One of his trusted assistants, Colin Bay, was coming along on the trip.

After successfully applying for a visa and receiving clearance for his work from the Nigerian high commission in London, the arachnoid man booked flights with British Airways for him and his assistant.

While preparing for the case, the arachnoid man read some books and conducted some Internet searches. He talked at length on the phone with the palace administrator to gain insight into the cultural setting in which the crime occurred, in the town of Ogan.

The arachnoid man and his assistant flew into Lagos, a large city in Nigeria, West Africa, arriving on a British Airways flight late in the evening. It was a hazy harmattan day, and it was mildly cold. In the arrival lounge, the palace administrator and his driver were waiting to receive them, with their names displayed on a piece of cardboard. As the arachnoid man emerged, the palace administrator instinctively sensed that the man was the one he was expecting. Walking toward the man, he said, "Good evening, sir. I am Ola Bada, the palace administrator. Are you the one I am expecting?"

With a firm handshake, the arachnoid man politely responded, "Yes, it is very kind of you to have come to welcome us." Ola Bada also greeted Colin Bay. After a few further exchanges of pleasantries, the driver collected their suitcases, wheeling them to a black jeep with the palace crest on the plate, parked in the VIP section.

The palace administrator opened the back door for the arachnoid man and his assistant while the driver, Mr. Bode, was loading the suitcases into the car.

As they drove down the motorway, the arachnoid man was intrigued by the beauty of the lush rainforest on either side. On their arrival at their hotel, two female receptionists, who were elegantly dressed, welcomed them with broad smiles and ushered them into their respective rooms. Departing for the night, the palace administrator wished them a good night's rest, adding that if they needed him, they could call his phone at any time.

The next day, the arachnoid man and Colin Bay woke up to a bright sunny day. They were scheduled to start interviewing the palace staff and family members after breakfast.

The first person to be interviewed was the first of the oba's four wives, Queen Moni. She was still dressed in black mourning clothing, as was the tradition. She walked into the beautiful, well-decorated, and large palace meeting hall with statues, traditional Yoruba carvings, bronze artifacts, and large paintings meticulously positioned all over.

As Queen Moni was led to her seat, she sat down quietly, acknowledging the arachnoid man's greetings with a gentle nod of her head.

Starting, the arachnoid man said, "Please accept my sincere condolences regarding the death of your husband, the oba. As you must have become well aware, the postmortem examination findings confirmed that he died of paraquat poisoning. The job of my team is to find who was responsible and bring him or her to justice. I believe that is a desire you share. Thus, our questioning will be thorough, scrutinizing, and intrusive and may touch on sensitive issues. We admonish you to bear with us."

Again Queen Moni nodded her head and said, "I understand. I am as committed as you are that the person responsible for the poisoning of my husband, Oba Adeke Olawumi, be apprehended and brought to justice, as suspicion has fallen on us, his wives, who prepare his meals. To tell you the truth, prior to his death, our relationship was less than cordial because I did not approve of the several additional wives. He married his second wife two years after our marriage. He promised me then that would be his last addition, but he never kept that promise.

"Nonetheless," continued Queen Moni, "he is my first love, and I never wanted him dead and would do nothing to harm him, though I had been refusing him sexual intimacy for about a year prior in rebellion. Now I wish I hadn't. I did not know his death was so close."

"To be clear," interjected the arachnoid man, "are you categorically saying that you are not responsible, you instructed no one and know nothing about the oba's poisoning?"

"Exactly. That is exactly what I am saying," replied Queen Moni in a raised voice. In a lower tone, she continued. "If my pushing him away by refusing sexual contact has anything remotely to do with his death, then that is a regret and guilt I will have to carry for the rest of my life and take to my grave.

"The oba had to marry a second wife because he liked bondage during sex and I was not into that. To be honest, on many occasions, their moaning, groaning, giggling, and excitement during their bondage sessions was very disturbing and kept me awake at times, as the wives' rooms are close to one another. Nonetheless, as I said earlier, I never wanted him dead."

"Judging from the onset of the symptoms prior to his death, his last meal was prepared by you," said the arachnoid man. "Can you please take me through the sequence of events during and after your preparation of his meal on that fateful day, until the meal reached the oba?"

Queen Moni adjusting her sitting position and her glasses and, speaking in a quiet, somber tone, replied, "After I finished preparing the white rice with red spicy stew and beef meat that day, I dished it into bowls as usual and put the bowls and his drinks of water and lemonade on a tray. By the time I finished doing this, the servant Peter, who usually takes the meals to the oba, was already waiting to carry it to him. The only thing that was different that day was that usually I would have to call Peter when the food was ready, but on that day he was already waiting. I thought nothing much of it, but following the incident, I wondered whether his eagerness on that day had an ulterior motive.

"I am not accusing Peter of anything. I am merely stating what happened surrounding the oba's last meal. Peter has served the oba's family faithfully for over twenty-five years. It is unfortunate that royalty does not immunize a man or woman against the vicissitudes of life."

"Where is Peter, that servant, now?" inquired the arachnoid man.

Responding, the palace administrator said, "Since the oba's passing away, he has been absent from work in the palace. He claims the oba's death has deeply affected him and that he is struggling to cope. We have directed him to go for counseling, and he has had a number of visits. The other servant, who has served the oba for more than thirty years, seems to be coping well and is currently at work."

"I will need to speak to both servants. Please kindly book them in the schedule as soon as possible," replied the arachnoid man.

The other wives were also interrogated, but none was considered a suspect.

Odu, one of the servants, attended the scheduled interviews at the appointed time, but Peter failed to show up for any of the meetings. He attributed it to being traumatized by the oba's sudden death, but suspicion began to arise when he turned down the alternative offer of the arachnoid man and his team coming to his house to conduct the interview.

Peter eventually appeared to be interviewed by the arachnoid man after receiving a letter from the palace administrator informing him that if he did not appear voluntarily, he would be forced to do so and would be interviewed under police caution. Thereafter, he appeared and then confessed to the involvement of the oba's son, Prince David, who was based in London, studying there. Peter produced a voice recording in which the oba's son, Prince David, gave him instructions about the use of the poison paraquat, which he put in the oba's food, mixing it with the red stew. Prince David's motives were that he wanted to ascend to the throne soon after the completion of his education and coming home from abroad. He also strongly felt that his father's leadership style was too lenient and old fashioned. The investigation further revealed an additional motive on the part of Prince David, who was the oba's second wife's son and next in line for the throne, as Queen Moni had only two daughters and only male children could ascend to the throne. Prince David had a secret affection for the oba's youngest wife, Georgina, who had a very beautiful figure and a lovely face. She was also an elegant, plump, well-educated, and fair-complexioned lady in the same age bracket as Prince David. He reckoned that if his plot was successful, she would be part of his inheritance.

Thereafter, Prince David was prosecuted and found guilty along with Peter.

The arachnoid man and Colin Bay returned to England to continue their work.

Six months later, it was seven weeks to the New York marathon, and the arachnoid man perceived by clairvoyance that a group of four men of North African origin based in the United States was planning bomb attacks during the marathon.

He contacted the FBI, whose representative flew to London to meet the arachnoid man to be fully briefed and collect more details about the planned attack.

The FBI agent was Stacy Cooper, an elegant, brilliant, tall blonde in her early thirties. On arrival at Heathrow Airport, the arachnoid man was waiting to pick her up and take her to the hotel booked for her.

As she emerged from arrival corridor, she walked elegantly and effortlessly as though gliding on her dark-brown high-heeled shoes while she pulled her long-handled silver suitcase along, with a black leather bag hanging down from her left shoulder.

The arachnoid man was captivated by her imposing presence from afar. He said to himself, "She looks like a sex bomb," suspecting she was the one he was waiting for as he held out a piece of paper with her name written on it.

Approaching the arachnoid man where he stood, she said with a gentle smile, "How can I help you, sir? I am Stacy Cooper."

With an outstretched right hand, the arachnoid man introduced himself and said, "I hope your journey was smooth. Let me have your suitcase. I will be taking you to the hotel booked for you."

After being checked into her room at the hotel, Stacy said to the arachnoid man, "As you are well aware, we have no time to waste, as I am due to fly back to the United States tomorrow. You told my chief that we need to act expeditiously to counter the terror attack, so can we start the briefing now?"

"Yes," replied the arachnoid man, "that is fine by me, provided you are not too tired to absorb the information."

"I am fine," said Stacy, making herself comfortable on the three-seater white leather sofa.

The arachnoid man pulled a chair toward himself, sat down, and started his narration.

"The group of four males in their twenties and thirties are all of North African descent, and they are terrorist sympathizers who have been groomed via the Internet. They have met together only once, in a café in central New York about six months ago, and they are deliberately avoiding much direct contact to avoid coming under suspicion. During their first meeting, they agreed on their coded language and have since been using it to communicate via text and e-mails. Their aim is to unleash massive carnage during the upcoming New York marathon, which is scheduled to take place in seven weeks.

"Terrorist One is the ringleader. He has been on your radar previously but has up until now been lying low, buying time. He is a psychopath and is very dangerous. On the day of the attack, he will emerge from his house dressed in camouflage and armed with a submachine gun. When approached, the marksmen must be prepared to shoot his hand to prevent him from reaching into his pocket and bag, which will be loaded with explosives.

"Terrorist Two is a diehard. He will be coming out of his parents' house in Clifford Avenue on that day with a red bag on his back. He is on a suicide mission and must be stopped at all costs.

"For Terrorists Three and Four, they are victims of indoctrination and are unwilling coerced individuals who are doing the bidding of their leader. They are not dangerous, and arresting them will provide valuable information and intelligence. In addition to the other confidential information I have provided to you, that should suffice, and assuming that your agency will conduct everything professionally, this terror plot should be successfully foiled. Failure to stop them is not an option."

Midway through the briefing, as Stacy was taking notes, she stood up and began pacing the hotel room while writing in shorthand.

The arachnoid man pleaded with her to sit down as her huge, supple bum was distracting his train of thought.

Stacy agreed to sit down and said, "I am happy you noticed, as after concluding the clean work, we will have to get down to the dirty but pleasant. I have read so much about your great sexual exploits and cannot wait to have a taste of them."

That comment was a pleasant surprise to the arachnoid man, who now remembered how he was admiring her from afar at the airport before she approached him as the person receiving her and taking her to the hotel.

Stacy inquired, "Is the coast clear? To be precise, what I mean is, I am free and single. Are you attached?"

"No, I am not at the moment," the arachnoid man quickly replied.

"Then let us get clear about confidentiality: all this stays in this room," said Stacy.

She reached for his jacket, removed it swiftly, and unbuckled his belt. Before he knew it, his trousers were off, and she was, with his help, sliding off his shirt and vest. "You have a strong physical and sexual presence as well as an alluring body," said Stacy as she undid her bra.

The passionate kisses began on the sofa, with the arachnoid man running his tongue through her lips into her mouth, then over her neck and ears, and later thrusting his well-sized cock in between her firm 42G boobs.

Then they transferred to the luxury double bed, where the arachnoid man, with a tongue guard in place, used his tongue to stimulate her clitoris in her well-shaved pussy, resulting in deep moaning sounds of ecstasy, laughter, and enjoyment. It became too much for Stacy to handle at that stage; thus, she asked him to stop the stimulation as she had become too sensitive.

She in turn gave him a powerful blow job with deep-throat thrusting for a moment; then he reverted to fingering her, stimulating her G-spot on her anterior vaginal wall before thrusting his fingers deep to swipe round her cervix and mobilize it from side to side, up and down, and backward and forward. This gave Stacy deep-seated arousal with a massive squirting orgasm, resulting in her wetting the towel in place underneath her.

Then came the moment when the arachnoid man was taking her from behind, doggy style, and massaging her supple, silky, and succulent bum. "Enjoying it?" he bellowed. "You are well endowed by the creator with a nice, elegant, good-to-feel butt." He rammed into her more and more, deepening the thrust of his rod and at the same time using his left middle finger to stimulate her clitoris from the front. The motions and emotions were explosive and ecstatic for both of them.

"It is one of my greatest assets, and I flaunt it and put it to good use," Stacy replied while moaning and wriggling at the same time.

The arachnoid man also stimulated Stacy by clitoral flipping, during which he used his index finger to flip her well-lubricated clitoral hood from side to side. This sent her into a new dimension of gasping excitement that she had never experienced. He ended the session with thumb thrusting, which Stacy claimed was new to her but was equally very well enjoyed. Now exhausted, they both lay on the bed naked and quiet for about ten minutes, after which they cleaned up and got dressed for a meal.

Stacy flew back to the United States to submit her report. While the arachnoid man was taking her to the airport the next day, they recounted the pleasant memories of the rancorous passions of the night before and lamented that it could not continue for much longer. With tear-laden eyes and a passionate hug, they bid each other good-bye. They were both happy and fulfilled that their paths in life had crossed.

The End

Quotations / Food for Thought

1. Sexual pleasure is one of the most enhancing pleasures of life. By enhancing it, we enhance life.

2. Many good relationships have been turned sour by sexual discontent or disharmony. Learn the power of sexual enjoyment and fulfillment.

3. Sexual prowess is a skill. Like any other skill, it can be learned and acquired.

4. Sex is neither vile nor foul; it is divine. It needs only to be illuminated by the intense light of knowledge, good skills, unselfishness, and open-mindedness.

5. As we lock the bedroom door, selfishness must be locked out during sex. Sex is for the mutual benefit of both.

6. Sexual health is as important as physical, mental, and spiritual health.

7. Taboos and prejudices are obstacles and hindrances to good sexual pleasure. What is yours?

8. Sex is not only meant for procreation; it is also meant to be enjoyed.

9. Men and women have equal inalienable rights to expect to enjoy sex.

10. The excitement of sex is unique; it catapults us into and beyond realms that we could not otherwise reach or achieve.

11. The sexual physiology of the genders differs. By seeking to understand it, we can optimize our enjoyment of sex.

12. Sexual energy should be well harnessed and directed to maximize sexual enjoyment.

13. To get into the fullness of the joy of sex, we need to pull down, disintegrate, and dismantle long-held cultural, social, and religious gender-discriminatory practices and barriers that foster servitude and inaccurate thinking. We need to raise our awareness and consciousness with regard to sexual legitimacy.

14. Sexual fulfillment enhances other aspects of life.

15. Be careful about making serious commitments or promises during the heat/excitement of sexual passion. It can result in ruination, as clear thinking is prevented by the fog of intense passion and pleasure.

16. In a relationship, sex should not be used as a weapon.

17. Though creed, culture, race, language, values, and understanding differ, the passion for and the enjoyment of sex is universal; it is a unifying influence in human experience. The language of sex is the same, symbolizing the universality of humanity and the need for it.

About the Author

Allen Matthews has worked in the health sector as a consultant, and he has extensive knowledge of male and female anatomy, physiology, psychology, and sexuality. He is passionate about spreading correct information about sex and helping others find sexual fulfillment and satisfaction.